MICHAEL GARLAND'S
Christmas Treasury

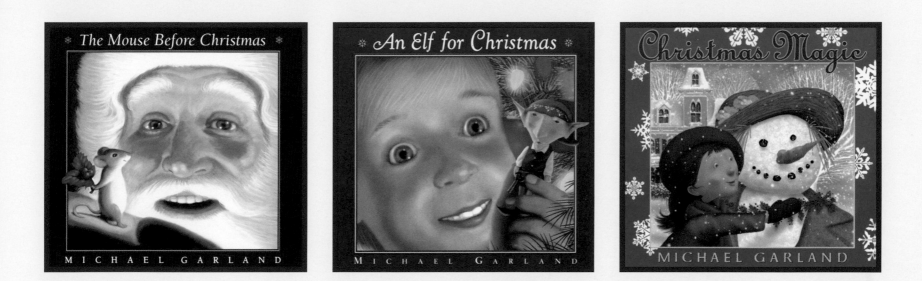

Dutton Children's Books

NEW YORK

Published in the United States by Dutton Children's Books,
a division of Penguin Young Readers Group
345 Hudson Street, New York, New York 10014
www.penguin.com

Manufactured in China

ISBN 0-525-47498-6

10 9 8 7 6 5 4 3 2 1

In our town, the day after Thanksgiving marked the beginning of preparations for Christmas. The ordinary was suddenly transformed into the exciting—colored lights were strung across the streets from telephone pole to telephone pole. Store windows were done up in red and green and sparkling tinsel. Shopping for the people on my little list with my little wallet was a merry treasure hunt.

As the big day approached, we drew Christmas pictures in school, made Christmas ornaments, and had Christmas parties. My Cub Scout troop marched from door to door, singing Christmas carols. The houses in my neighborhood sparkled with lights, and glowing trees peeked through each living-room window. My mother made her special Christmas cookies, and I would eat mountains of them. By the time Christmas Eve rolled around, I was so wound up I couldn't sit down, let alone sleep! Something wonderful, something magical was about to happen.

That's the feeling I try to capture in my books: a mouse takes a trip around the world with Santa, an elf flies a toy plane to the North Pole, snow people come to life. Such stories capture the imagination most at Christmastime—when fantasy and reality easily blur. I hope that reading these tales together will add to your family's joy this Christmas and for many holiday seasons to come.

Michael Garland

The Mouse Before Christmas

MICHAEL GARLAND

MICHAEL GARLAND

The Mouse Before Christmas

DUTTON CHILDREN'S BOOKS   NEW YORK

Library of Congress Cataloging-in-Publication Data

Garland, Michael, date
The mouse before Christmas/Michael Garland.—1st ed.
p. cm.
Summary: On Christmas Eve, a little mouse decides to stay awake to see Santa and
ends up taking a wild ride in Santa's sleigh before being returned home safe and sound.
ISBN 0-525-45578-7 (HC)
[1. Mice—Fiction. 2 Christmas—Fiction. 3. Santa Claus—Fiction.
4. Stories in rhyme.] I. Title.
PZ8.3.G185Mo 1997
[E]—dc21 96-50156 CIP AC

Published in the United States 1997 by Dutton Children's Books,
a division of Penguin Books USA Inc.
375 Hudson Street, New York, New York 10014

Designed by Riki Levinson
Manufactured in China   First Edition
5 7 9 10 8 6

To Katie, Alice, and Kevin

On the night before Christmas, there was a young mouse
Who was stirring and whirling all through the house.
He longed to see Santa (that jolly old soul),
So he'd stayed awake late and then crept from his hole.

He soon spied a place to poke his head free,
Then beheld all around him sights splendid to see.
He was high above Earth in the winter night sky,
Streaking past stars in a sleigh that could fly.
Mouse loved this new feeling, and when he looked down,
Far distant below shone the lights of his town.

Over bridges and castles and towers they flew;
The rooftops of London gave Mouse a great view.

Thrilling sights waited in each foreign land.
In Holland the windmills by moonlight looked grand.

Mouse had never imagined a world so wide;
He lost count of the wonders he'd seen on this ride—

Crossing cities and countries, over desert and sea,
Past the sphinx and two towers and Miss Liberty.

Santa just chuckled. "Little friend, don't you worry!
Hop on my hat. You'll be home in a hurry."
Mouse clung to the fringe—the wind chilled his face.
The rocketlike sleigh zoomed and hurtled through space.

Back home, safe and sound, there were presents for all.
The one Mouse liked best was a hat marked size SMALL.
Then Santa crouched down till his beard touched the floor.
The friends waved good-bye through the little front door.

On this busy Christmas Eve, the whole workshop was filled with the noise of hammering, sawing, and sanding. Teams of elves painted and stitched, glued and carved, rushing to finish the toys that Santa would deliver. The clock had already struck eleven, and the gifts still had to be wrapped and loaded onto the sleigh.

had
long
get b

At last, they reached Santa's workshop. As Tingle slid to the ground, the door burst open and Santa, Mrs. Claus, and all the elves spilled out.

"Hurrah! Tingle is back!" they shouted. "Welcome home, Tingle!"

The elves gave the bear some fish and thanked him for helping their friend. Then Tingle went inside to enjoy the Christmas dinner they had saved for him. In between bites, he told the elves his tale of daring adventure.

"I'm proud of you, Tingle," said Santa. "I knew you wouldn't forget our old saying, 'If there's no one around to help an elf, an elf should help himself.'"

"You've had a very busy Christmas," Santa said. "Why don't you go on to bed and get some sleep."

"Soon," said Tingle. "But right now there's *one* more thing I have to do."

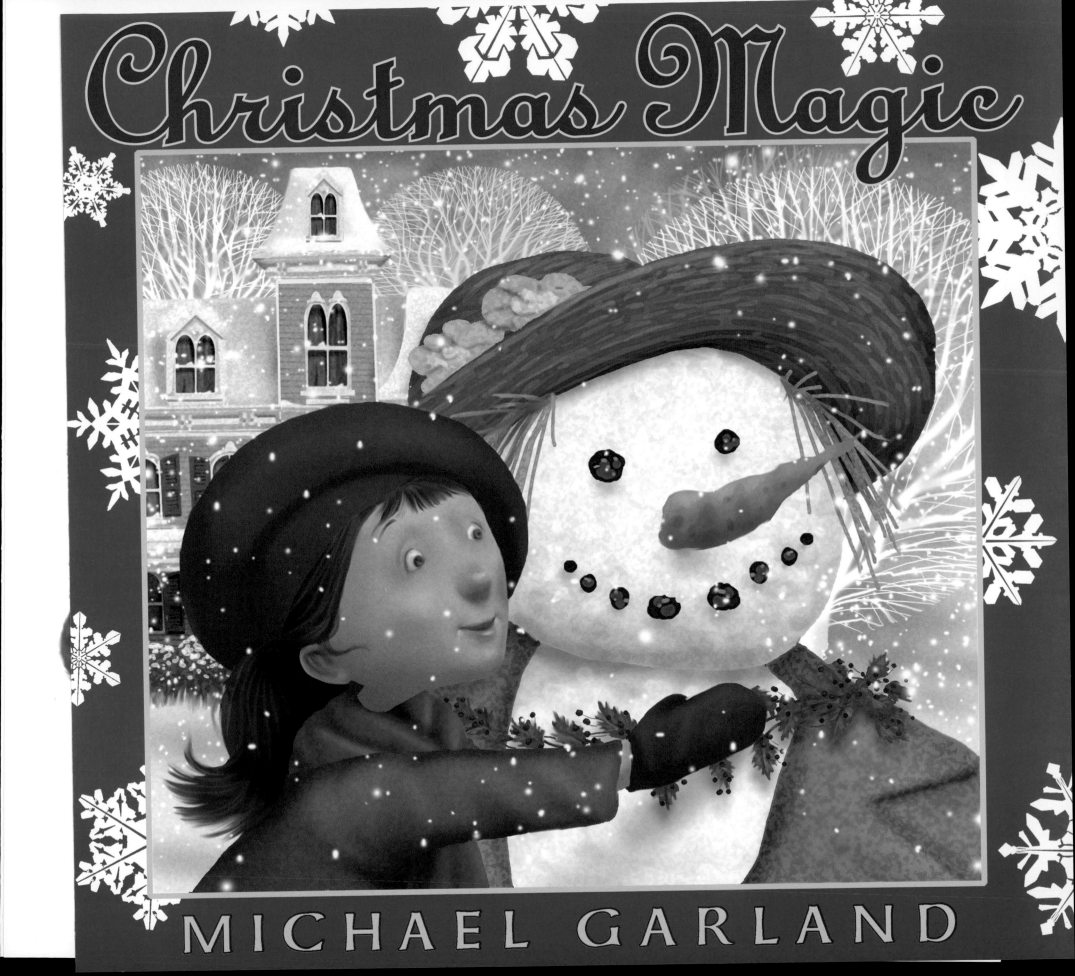

Christmas Magic

MICHAEL GARLAND

Emily had always loved Christmas Eve, but this year something about it felt different. She couldn't tell quite what—maybe it was the way the snow glittered and danced as it drifted down from the sky. It seemed to her that the snowflakes had never been so perfect.

She watched the boy who was moving in next door. He seemed too shy to even say hello. A new friend would be nice, she thought, but he went inside before she could think of what to say.

Emily continued to roll the snowball she was forming and tried to imagine how her snow-woman would look when she was done.

Once inside, she carried her gifts—already wrapped and ribboned—to their place under the tree. Emily had finished her Christmas shopping weeks ago. She had picked out something special for Mother, Father, her cat, Ginger, and Max, her dog.

Next, she lifted the delicate angel choir from a cardboard box and carefully placed each figure on the round table. She glanced with anticipation at the empty stockings and then went upstairs to her room.

Katrina and the snowman weren't just looking at each other now—they were turning into real people! Of all the magical things Emily had seen, this was by far the most amazing. The snowman walked over to Katrina and bowed. She answered with a graceful curtsy.

Emily watched the dashing couple swoop and swirl over the glittering snow.
In one last sweep, they danced to the steps of her house.

Emily heard a light knocking and ran to the door. She was so excited she could hardly open it. There stood Katrina, radiant in her snowy gown. Emily smiled up at her.

"Hello, Emily," said Katrina. "We thought you might like to come outside and dance with us."

Emily nodded eagerly, then quickly put on her hat and coat, mittens, and boots.

Katrina and the snowman each took one of Emily's hands, and they leaped and swayed and twirled together over the moonlit snow.

When the snow stopped falling and dawn was near, Katrina looked up at the brightening sky. Emily followed her gaze.

"I loved dancing with you," Emily said breathlessly. "But I should go home now. Thank you for inviting me."

"Merry Christmas. We will never forget you," said Katrina, squeezing Emily's hand tightly in her own.

Once inside, Emily found she was too tired to climb the stairs. She snuggled up in the big chair by the Christmas tree and was soon fast asleep.

The next thing Emily knew, she felt a gentle shaking. She sat up and looked around in bewilderment. The stockings hung peacefully above the fireplace. The angels stood exactly where she had placed them.

"Did the mice finish baking the pies?" she asked.

Father laughed. "That must have been some dream!"

Maybe I *did* dream the whole thing, she thought. There's only one way to find out.

Emily pulled on her coat over her nightgown and ran outside.

There, side by side on the sparkling snow, stood Katrina and the snowman.
The boy from next door was there, too.

"I can't believe it!" he whispered. "How did my snowman get all the way
over here?"

Emily grinned at him. "It was the Christmas magic," she whispered back.

Katrina and the snowman didn't say anything, but Emily was sure their
smiles were even wider than before.